Molly
the
Pirate

For my granddaughter, Nathalie LT
To all our salty inland pirates PS

Molly the Pirate

Illustrated by

Lorraine Teece

Paul Seden

Magabala
BOOKS

Molly lived a long way from the sea, but every day she wished she was a pirate.

and her eye patch,

and she tucked her sword into her belt.

She put on her pirate hat

She pushed her boat into the choppy sea

and rowed out
to the pirate ship.

Molly leapt onto the deck and cried,
'Hello salty buccaneers, I'm Molly. Look at what I can do!'

Molly walked the plank
and drew her sword
at Captain Chicken.

She did back flips and front flips

up and down the deck.

She danced a jolly jig
in front of the dazed
captain and his crew.

She scrambled up the rigging
and shouted, 'Look at me,
I can touch the clouds!'

When the hungry pirates sat down to eat, she politely asked, 'May I have some please?'

After lunch, Molly took the wheel and steered the pirate ship towards the shore.

It was time to row home and rest before her next pirate adventure.

'Wake up sleepyhead,
let's have lunch',
laughed Molly's mum.

Molly didn't tell her mum
she had already eaten.

Lorraine Teece is an Elder of the Alayawarra people from Central Australia. Along with her academic achievements, she has written and illustrated many children's books. Lorraine is an award-winning artist. She lives in Southern Queensland and finds her inspiration in the landscape of the Australian outback.

Paul Seden is descended from the Wuthagthi and Muralag people of North Queensland. He grew up in Darwin where he lives with his family. Paul loves to draw and create stories about real and imaginary characters. His book *Crabbing with Dad* was shortlisted in the Small Publishers' Children's Book of the Year, ABIA Awards 2017.

First published 2017 by Magabala Books Aboriginal Corporation, Broome, Western Australia
Website: www.magabala.com   Email: sales@magabala.com

Magabala Books receives financial assistance from the Commonwealth Government through the Australia Council, its arts advisory body. The State of Western Australia has made an investment in this project through the Department of Culture and the Arts in association with LotteryWest. Magabala Books would like to acknowledge the generous support of the Shire of Broome, Western Australia.

Paul Seden was supported by the Australian Indigenous Creator Scholarships, a Magabala Books initiative that offers professional development through its philanthropic fund.

Designed by Jo Hunt
Colour reproduction by Splitting Image Colour Studio Pty Ltd
Printed in China by Toppan Leefung Printing Ltd

Cataloguing-in-Publication Data available from the National Library of Australia